BOOK CLUB IN A BOX

Bookclub-in-a-Box presents the discussion companion for Philip Roth's novel

The Human Stain

Published by Vintage International, 2000, a division of Random House Incorporated. ISBN: 0-375-72634-9

Quotations used in this guide have been taken from the text of the paperback edition of **The Human Stain**. All information taken from other sources is acknowledged.

This discussion companion for **The Human Stain** has been prepared and written by Marilyn Herbert, originator of Bookclub-in-a-Box. Marilyn Herbert. B.Ed., is a teacher, librarian, speaker and writer. Bookclub-in-a-Box is a unique guide to current fiction and classic literature intended for book club discussions, educational study seminars, and personal pleasure. For more information about the Bookclub-in-a-Box team, visit our website.

Bookclub-in-a-Box discussion companion for The Human Stain

ISBN 10: 0-9733984-4-2
ISBN 13: 9780973398441

This guide reflects the perspective of the Bookclub-in-a-Box team and is the sole property of Bookclub-in-a-Box.

©2005 BOOKCLUB-IN-A-BOX
©2008 NEW EDITION - OC

Unauthorized reproduction of this book or its contents for republication in whole or in part is strictly prohibited.

CONTACT INFORMATION: SEE BACK COVER.

CONTENTS

BOOKCLUB-IN-A-BOX
Philip Roth's The Human Stain

READERS AND LEADERS GUIDE 2

INTRODUCTION
- Suggested Beginnings 7
- Novel Quickline 8
- Keys to the Novel 9

CHARACTERIZATION
- Coleman 14
- Les 15
- Faunia 16
- Delphine 17
- Zuckerman 19

FOCUS POINTS AND THEMES
- Human Condition 24
- Secrets 25
- Identity 26
- Judgment 27
- Revenge 28
- Society 29
- Sex 30
- Power of Language 31

WRITING STRUCTURE
- The First 85 pages 35
- Greek Drama 37

SYMBOLS
- Human Stain 43
- Labels 45
- Prince, the Crow 46
- The Dance 47

WRITING STYLE
- Wordplay 51
- Narrator (Nathan Zuckerman) 54

LAST THOUGHTS
- Author Background 59
- The Other Roth 63
- Works by Roth 65
- Other Characters 67

FROM THE NOVEL (QUOTES) ... 81

ACKNOWLEDGEMENTS 87

BOOKCLUB-IN-A-BOX
Readers and Leaders Guide

Each Bookclub-in-a-Box guide is clearly and effectively organized to give you information and ideas for a lively discussion, as well as to present the major highlights of the novel. The format, with a Table of Contents, allows you to pick and choose the specific points you wish to talk about. It does not have to be used in any prescribed order. In fact, it is meant to support, not determine, your discussion.

You Choose What to Use.

You may find that some information is repeated in more than one section and may be cross-referenced so as to provide insight on the same idea from different angles.

The guide is formatted to give you extra space to make your own notes.

How to Begin

Relax and look forward to enjoying your bookclub.

With Bookclub-in-a-Box as your behind the scenes support, there is little for you to do in the way of preparation.

Some readers like to review the guide after reading the novel; some before. Either way, the guide is all you will need as a companion for your discussion. You may find that the guide's interpretation, information, and background have sparked other ideas not included.

Having read the novel and armed with Bookclub-in-a-Box, you will be well prepared to lead or guide or listen to the discussion at hand.

Lastly, if you need some more 'hands-on' support, feel free to contact us. (See Contact Information)

What to Look For

Each Bookclub-in-a-Box guide is divided into easy-to-use sections, which include points on characters, themes, writing style and structure, literary or historical background, author information, and other pertinent features unique to the novel being discussed. These may vary slightly from guide to guide.

INTERPRETATION OF EACH NOVEL REFLECTS THE PERSPECTIVE OF THE BOOKCLUB-IN-A-BOX TEAM.

Do We Need to Agree?
THE ANSWER TO THIS QUESTION IS NO.

If we have sparked a discussion or a debate on certain points, then we are happy. We invite you to share your group's alternative findings and experiences with us. You can respond on-line at our website or contact us through our Contact Information. We would love to hear from you.

Discussion Starters

There are as many ways to begin a bookclub discussion as there are members in your group. If you are an experienced group, you will already have your favorite ways to begin. If you are a newly formed group or a group looking for new ideas, here are some suggestions.

Ask for people's impressions of the novel. (This will give you some idea about which parts of the unit to focus on.)

- Identify a favorite or major character.
- Identify a favorite or major idea.
- Begin with a powerful or pertinent quote. (not necessarily from the novel)
- Discuss the historical information of the novel. (not applicable to all novels)
- If this author is familiar to the group, discuss the range of his/her work and where this novel stands in that range.
- Use the discussion topics and questions in the Bookclub-in-a-Box guide.

If you have further suggestions for discussion starters, be sure to share them with us and we will share them with others.

Above All, Enjoy Yourselves

INTRODUCTION

Suggested Beginnings

Novel Quickline

Keys to the Novel

INTRODUCTION

Suggested Beginnings

1. The structure of Roth's novel is peculiar and may strike first-time readers as disconcerting.

How does Roth connect the historical events in the first section to the story of his fictional characters? What greater parallel is Roth trying to draw between the people of the past and the present, and how is this related to the concept of the "human stain"?

2. Many find Roth's writing verbose and confusing. The relationship of an author to his work is not explicit because Roth does not write with his readers in mind. Instead, he writes for the benefit of his own self-exploration, a fact which is evident in his stream-of-consciousness style.

How does Roth use the characters to explore issues directly affecting him, such as religious and cultural assimilation? Discuss Roth's interconnected relationship with Nathan Zuckerman.

4. Consider the significance of the image of the "human stain" in light of popular culture and mass media.

How does Roth use the Clinton/Lewinsky scandal of 1998 to illustrate this point?

5. The power of language is an important element in the novel.

Discuss Roth's views about the misuse of language as well as the importance of words and labels to human behavior and progress.

6. Philip Roth has an extraordinary ability to layer irony; the character Nelson Primus is a good example.

Consider whether Primus is black or white. Discuss the clues that Roth lays down to demonstrate this irony.

Novel Quickline

Coleman Silk is an all-American success story. Born to working class parents and raised in Newark, New Jersey, Coleman goes on to be a star athlete, does his military service in the navy, graduates with honors from university, and becomes a professor of classic literature at Athena College. He marries Iris Gittelman and has four children, who also achieve successful professional careers.

All of this takes place before the book opens. By the time we meet Coleman, his life is in shambles: Iris is dead, his children are no longer speaking to him, he has left his post at the university under ignominious circumstances, and he is having an affair with a much younger woman, whose ex-husband is trying to kill him.

How and why this occurs and what this has to do with ex-President Bill Clinton is fascinating reading.

Keys to the Novel

Philip Roth's two favorite topics are the human condition and the craft of writing. These topics are repeated in every novel in Roth's extensive bibliography of works. Philip Roth continually finds new ways of presenting these topics, even while using the same characters, such as Nathan Zuckerman.

Identity

- Who we are as individuals, as members of our individual communities and as members of the general community of the human race are the central issues of the human condition that concern Coleman Silk, Nathan Zuckerman, and Philip Roth. Here, in the novel, identity makes its appearance both as a major theme and a dilemma.

- Philip Roth has invented the characters of Coleman Silk and Nathan Zuckerman. There is confusion as to whether these characters are separate and individual creations of imagination or whether they represent autobiographical and unique aspects of the real person, Philip Roth. Each of these three is consumed with questions about personal, cultural, and human identity. They provide observations, not solutions.

- In Roth's novels, the question of the author's personality and identity is the same: who is the real Philip Roth and who is the invention?
(see Nathan Zuckerman, p.19)

Writing

- Philip Roth is a master of language. Where other authors use language as a microscope to clarify or isolate a single idea, Roth uses a single word, sentence, or paragraph as a prism, thereby reflecting his ideas differently according to the angle of the prism. In this way, he proposes a number of different observations that the reader can accept, reject, or add to. The reader becomes part of Roth's writing experience. (Of course, you have to like long, convoluted sentences that digress in a stream-of-consciousness kind of way.)

CHARACTERIZATION

Coleman

Les

Faunia

Delphine

Zuckerman

CHARACTERIZATION

All of Philip Roth's characters are unique and unforgettable. There is not one superfluous character in the entire book. However, if we were forced to choose the key characters, they would be Coleman, Farley, Faunia, Delphine and Zuckerman. The rest are very active supports for these five and must be considered in that light.

This section will deal with the key characters but will include interesting details and thoughts about the supporting cast. (For Other Characters, see p.67)

Coleman Silk

- Coleman is a fighter, literally and figuratively. He begins boxing at the age of fourteen with Doc Chizner at the Newark Boys Club; he fights while he's in university and in the navy. He continues to be confrontational even when he becomes Dean at Athena College. Although he is not an altruistic idealist, Coleman hires a multiracial and multiethnic staff: Blacks, Jews, and Frenchmen. He brings to the college healthy competition that later, for him, has unfortunate and unhealthy results. But perhaps he does it also because he enjoys the irony:

   > *Coleman was not ... fighting for integration and equality and civil rights ... he was never fighting for anything other than himself .... In it always for Coleman alone. All he ever wanted was out.* (p.324)

- Essentially, Coleman is fighting for the right to receive his fair share of the American Dream. He appears to be successful: he is a national athlete; a straight-A student; is good-looking; and has a successful, feisty wife and four healthy kids. He is a self-made man, and all he wants is the freedom to pursue his choice of identity. There is only one problem: he's black.

- In order to defy his destiny he must change it, so he tries to stretch and escape the limits set for him by the reality of his life as a black American in the forties and fifties. He does this by adopting a secret life as a Jew. But as the Bible says,

   > *Pride goeth before destruction, and an haughty spirit before a fall.* Proverbs 16:18

   Pride is Coleman's downfall.

- For Coleman, the idea of having a secret is a key to understanding him: first he hides his fights from his father; then he falsifies his age in order to enter the navy. Following this, he re-labels his racial identity; and finally he assumes a completely fake and secret life.

- Ernestine, Coleman's sister, points out that Coleman didn't suffer the intolerance that his father suffered. She does not excuse Coleman's outrageous behavior on the basis of his having been a victim of racial prejudice, but rather she understands that for Coleman the world is a bigger place, where boundary lines can be blurred. For Coleman, the world is a stage where he can act any way he wants:

    > ... *people grow up and go away and have nothing to do with their families ever again, and they don't have to be colored to act like that ...* (p.325)

Les Farley

- Unlike Coleman, Les Farley is a visibly confrontational man. He has served his country twice in Vietnam. When he returns, he marries Faunia and they have two children, who die under terrible circumstances. He tries his hand at farming, but he really can't handle the pressures of his life. He suffers terribly from war-related, post-traumatic stress. Like Coleman, he also seeks the benefits of the American dream: the freedom to be who he wants to be – to be successful, respected, and appreciated. Unfortunately, Farley is not successful – he has no professional stature and no warm home and hearth. Farley is a husband, father, farmer, road-crew worker, war veteran, and failure. He *"had not meant to fail, but did."* (p.64)

- Farley is a fighter with knee-jerk reactions, who sees the world in black-and-white terms, whereas Coleman tries to see it in full color. Through Farley, we are introduced to the idea of payback and justice for a multitude of sins, including the sin of pride. (see Revenge, p.28)

- Farley, like Coleman, is a man in search of an identity. He becomes a farmer only because his friend, Kenny (who died in Vietnam), had been a farmer. While Coleman struggles with the effort of falsely presenting himself, Farley struggles against other people's false perceptions of him:

  > ... *they're all afraid of him .... They see him coming and they think he is going to steal the kids .... He's just a crazy Vietnam vet.* (p.64, 68)

Faunia Farley

- Faunia, Coleman's mistress, is almost the complete opposite of Coleman. She is white, blond, and has a gaunt appearance that is a testament to her hard life, as opposed to Coleman, who lives a life of relative privilege. She works at the college as a cleaner; he, as the dean.

- She is not a fighter like Coleman and does not even defend herself against her ex-husband, Farley. In a sense, she suffers from a different kind of pride, one that compels her to hide the reality of her identity. Her blanket acceptance of every demeaning obstacle that life has placed in her path—including death—is her way of continually punishing herself for the death of her children; it is her payback.

- Faunia does have one thing in common with Coleman in that she has a secret: a diary. She hides the fact of her literacy from the world. By hiding behind a facade, Faunia illustrates that even illiteracy can be a form of power if you need it. And like Coleman's false identity, Faunia's illiteracy *"spices things up."* (p.297)

- Coleman names the plain Faunia his *Voluptas*. (p.116) In the mythology of the Ancient Romans, Voluptas is the personification of sensual pleasure; for Coleman, Faunia is the same. Coleman also gives this name to Steena, but never to his wife, Iris.

Delphine Roux

- Delphine, the dean of the Classics Department, was recruited and hired to Athena by Coleman when he was the dean of the college. Delphine has two purposes in the novel. First, her constant obsession with who she is induces us to look at the concept of identity. Delphine attempts to redefine her identity by moving to another country: *"I will go to America and be the author of my life."* (p.273)

- Delphine would probably have been a happier person had she stayed in France, but she couldn't see it at the time. Her name, Delphine, is an ironic choice that reminds us of the Greek oracle at Delphi, but unlike her namesake, she is unable to predict the loneliness, isolation, and frustration of the experiences she will encounter. She is simultaneously *"afraid of being exposed, dying to be seen – there's a dilemma for you."* (p.185)

- Second, through Delphine's actions, we are asked to consider how a single action can innocently set a whole avalanche of events into motion. Her last name, Roux, is a French cooking term. Flour is blended into oil or melted butter – this is the roux. When this is added to a sauce, it changes the nature of the sauce. Delphine, as well as Farley, show how singular acts can change the direction of life in an instant.

- Delphine certainly sets in motion a series of events that changes Coleman's life and possibly leads to his death. Delphine is responsible for the anonymous letter that Coleman receives that exposes his secret relationship with Faunia: *"Everyone knows you're sexually exploiting an abused, illiterate woman half your age."* (p.38) If we follow the ripples back to when Coleman receives this note, we know that he begs Zuckerman to help him fight his last fight. Ironically, Coleman wants the truth out in the open in order to tell his story and clear his name, but the truth he wants to tell is not the truth about who he really is.

- Preoccupied with herself at the time of Coleman's death, Delphine accidentally emails her ad for a man (for Coleman) to the faculty at the college instead of to The *New York Times*. Realizing her mistake, Delphine attempts to cover up by ransacking her own office and claiming that Coleman was responsible for the mess and for the email hoax. She doesn't back down even when she learns that he and Faunia have died. Her life has spun into *"a drama beyond her control."* (p.273)

- This ripple effect is completed when Nathan discovers an anonymous on-line eulogy for Faunia. He deduces that Delphine could not have written this because the tone of the note was not petty, contrived, or nasty.

    > *... this was mischief, more than likely, prompted by Delphine's mischief, but more artful, more confident, more professionally demonic by far – a major upgrade of the venom. And what would it now inspire? Where would this public stoning stop? Where would the gullibility stop?* (p.289)

Nathan Zuckerman

- Nathan Zuckerman first appeared in Roth's writings in **The Ghost Writer** and reappeared in seven more novels, including **The Human Stain**. He quickly became a favorite of Roth's and is his alter-ego, or "alter-brain" as Roth likes to call him. (McGrath) Like Roth, Zuckerman is a controversial novelist, and through Zuckerman Roth can say and do anything. (see Author, p.59) In fact, in **The Facts**, Roth's autobiographical book, he quotes the fictional Zuckerman:

    And as he spoke I was thinking [of] the kind of stories that people turn life into, the kind of lives that people turn stories into.

- In **The Human Stain**, Zuckerman, Coleman's neighbor and acquaintance, is the narrator of Coleman's story, literally and fictionally. Roth intentionally blurs the lines between reality and fiction and brings the issue of credibility to the forefront. As readers, we are being asked to decide who and what we can really believe. (see Narrator, p.54)

    I had to write something for him—he all but ordered me to. If he wrote the story in all of its absurdity ... nobody would believe it ... But if I wrote it, if a professional writer wrote it ... (p.11)

For more information about Nathan Zuckerman, see Narrator, p.54.

FOCUS POINTS AND THEMES

Human Condition

Secrets

Identity

Judgment

Revenge

Society

Sex

Power of Language

FOCUS POINTS AND THEMES

In a discussion of the focal points and central ideas in Roth's novel, it is important to note that **The Human Stain** is the last book of a trilogy: **American Pastoral, I Married a Communist,** and **The Human Stain.** The trilogy spans the latter half of the twentieth century and deals with the moral and ethical sides of political and human behavior in connection to America's involvement in the Vietnam War, the McCarthy communist witch hunts, and the impeachment of a president for a crime no one cared about. **The Human Stain** sums up the century's faults and foibles by dealing with our common heritage – the propensity for human error and self-righteous judgment of others, a characteristic that marks (or stains) us as uniquely human. It is Roth's view on this human condition that is the central focus point of the novel.

In the opening of **The Human Stain**, Roth introduces us to Coleman in his classroom, where he begins the school term by discussing a Greek myth that describes a bitter quarrel over a young girl between *"Agamemnon the King of men, and great Achilles."* (p.4) Coleman teaches this myth as the example that began the tradition of *"the great imaginative literature of Europe ... and that is why, close to three thousand years later, we are going to begin there today..."* (p.5)

Roth offers no solutions, just observations. He wonders why, if we know so much about ourselves, human nature has not changed since the beginning of recorded human history; we exhibit the same behaviors now as we see in the Bible or in a Greek drama.

Human Condition

- Roth sees our flawed behavior as the essence of our humanity, and his term, the human stain, refers to this flawed behavior. The idea of the mark/stain is taken from the story of Adam and Eve in the Garden of Eden and from the story of Cain and Abel. Adam and Eve are marked by being eternally banished into an imperfect world outside the garden. Cain is literally and forever "stained" by God for his act of murder.

- The Greeks also used this idea and went one step further by hiding the marks of one's character, emotions, or history behind a mask. The idea of a mask is very important because it influences the perceptions others have about us.

- Throughout the novel Roth uses both the Biblical image and the symbol of the mask to show how the characters protect their real identities from the judgments of others. Faunia hides behind the mask of illiteracy. Coleman hides behind his Jewish mask. Coleman's son, Mark, by his very name and by his anger, symbolizes the crack in Coleman's mask.

FOCUS POINTS AND THEMES

- Roth explores why people feel the need to hide or present themselves falsely. While he looks at the common human behaviors of his characters and their actions, he explores why people are judgmental and sanctimonious. By including references to the impeachment of President Bill Clinton, Roth also takes a direct shot at American society in order to remind us that, after all, it is simply *"A HUMAN BEING [who] LIVES HERE."* (p.3)

Secrets

It is a uniquely human trait to use a secret to cover up something we consider shameful or undesirable. According to psychologists, philosophers, and writers, secrets are indelible marks that stain our psyches, and secrets have a habit of coming back to haunt us.

- Coleman has a secret life and likes it. He finds secrecy – the idea of getting away with something – exhilarating. (see Coleman, p.14) When Coleman marries Iris, he finds *"the secret to his secret, flavored with just a drop of the ridiculous ... life's little contribution to every human decision .... he now made sense."* (p.132)

    > *... it's the secret that's his [Coleman's] magnetism ... the enigmatic it that he holds apart as his and no one else's. He's set himself up like the moon to be only half visible.* (p.213)

- He only comes close to admitting his secret to Iris after the birth of their fourth child, when he is relieved to realize that he has indeed gotten away with his racial deception: there is no mark of Coleman's black identity on any of his children. He never gets the chance to tell her, and ironically Iris is *"the only woman never to know his secret."* (p.337)

- Steena, Ellie, Faunia, Coleman's mother, and his sister all know he has a secret. Almost everyone, including Zuckerman, knows, but it is not yet clear what that secret is.

- In fact, when Delphine writes in a note to Coleman, "*Everyone knows,*" (p.38) referring to his affair with Faunia, we are initially confused. After all, he is not committing adultery or any other real crime. What we don't know at the time is that Coleman is afraid, in fact, that "everything" about him is about to be exposed.

- Secrets take on a life of their own and can (and do in this novel) grow beyond one's control. *"As it is a human thing to have a secret, it is also a human thing, sooner or later, to reveal it."* (p.337, 338) Dostoevsky wrote about this in **Crime and Punishment**, and, in this novel, it is Delphine who illustrates this idea. Her actions concerning Coleman grow beyond her and she has to create a bigger crisis (she ransacks her own office) in order to cover up the smaller ones (her email about Coleman).

Masking Our Identities

It is human nature to try and present ourselves as better than we really are in order to prevent exposing our inner vulnerability. While Roth presents the true identities of his characters to the reader, his characters misrepresent themselves to each other. Roth plays with the notion that a false appearance is like a mask; it hides what is beneath. (see Greek Drama, p.37)

- There are active and passive masks. Faunia hides her real self behind a mask of illiteracy; Delphine changes continents in an effort to change people's perceptions of her. Poor Farley tries hard but cannot change anyone's perceptions of him. Ironically, it is Nelson Primus who isn't hiding anything and is startled by Coleman's misconception of who he (Primus) really is. Finally, there is Coleman, who passively allows people to come to their own conclusions about his Jewishness and who never bothers to correct them.

- In a manner as smooth as silk, Roth actually "outs" Coleman right at the novel's beginning: Coleman is a handsome man, "the small-nosed Jewish type" with a name that doesn't *"give him away as a Jew – because it could as easily have been a Negro's name."* (p.15, 16) But, Roth tells us, some people are not misled, and we learn that on one occasion, Coleman had attempted to enter a brothel. His ejection from the brothel illustrates his identity dilemma: he is *"[thrown] out of a Norfolk whorehouse for being black, thrown out of Athena College for being white."* (p.16)

The Leap to Judgment

For Roth, personal identity is so complex, and flaws so universal, that there should be no place for the judging or labeling of others. This human propensity for judgment should lead us to see how easily we betray others and how easily, therefore, we can be betrayed. But alas, like Roth's characters, we rarely take the insight that far.

- Everyone's character in the novel passes judgment on everyone else in an effort to feel better about him or herself: Delphine and Coleman's children pass judgment on Faunia; Coleman passes judgment on Farley; Farley passes judgment on Faunia; and everyone passes judgment on Coleman. And just in case we miss the point, Roth throws in the real and up-to-date story of former president Bill Clinton and Monica Lewinsky to see by what criteria we, the real participants in world history, judge others. We could and perhaps should ask, **How would we have judged Coleman if we had known the truth of who he was?**

Was the idea he [Coleman] had for himself of lesser validity or of greater validity than someone else's idea of what he was supposed to be? Can such things even be known? (p.333)

Revenge, Retribution

Ill-conceived judgments create a ripple effect that extends beyond our control. Much of it ends up as *"payback."* (p.67)

- As seen in the novel, there is the purposeful and direct vengeance wrought by Farley in reaction to his perception of Faunia's behavior.

    He'd made up his mind. Use his vehicle. Take them all out, including himself. Along the river, come right at them, in the same lane, in their lane, round the turn where the river bends. (p.256)

- There is also the indirect vengefulness of Delphine in reaction to her unrequited feelings for Coleman. In both cases, the results are significant and catastrophic.

- It is Coleman alone who feels that life should offer more than a repetitious cycle of human revenge and retribution. One has to *"learn ... before you die, to live beyond the jurisdiction of their enraging, loathsome, stupid blame."* (p.64) Otherwise, the payback is certain and eternal.

The Individual in Society
responsibility and inclusion

It is impossible to live in isolation, but in the novel everyone tries. Roth shows how isolation has its consequences whether one isolates oneself or is isolated by others. Coleman isolates himself from his family, and this action has consequences. When society ostracizes Farley, there are also consequences.

- Nathan tries to live quietly and independently outside of the community while recovering from prostate surgery. He leaves New York and *"move[s] into a two-room cabin set way back in a field on a rural road high in the Berkshires [where he doesn't have to] meet new people or ... join a new community."* (p.10) It is Coleman who pulls him back into the center. It is tempting for Nathan to stay isolated, but he finds out that on the human stage this is impossible: *"I did no more than find a friend, and all the world's malice came rushing in."* (p.45) Zuckerman recognizes that while the individual may seek personal freedom, there is a parallel demand from the community at large that may infringe on that search.

- On the other hand, Farley wants to belong, but it is the community that keeps pushing him out because he has *"wreak[ed] havoc"* (p.65) in Vietnam. Now *"he really doesn't belong ... he feels that he is no longer a part of their world ... he cannot connect to them and they cannot connect to him."* (p.66) Roth is not talking about forgiveness but of understanding. He asserts that even the person whose behavior is on the fringe of acceptability should be recognized as part of our common humanity.

- Ironically Roth himself has been heavily criticized for seeming to lack "Jewishness" and for failing in his responsibility to the Jewish community. (see The Other Roth, p.63) Even more ironic is that in this novel Roth takes the ideal of humanity and its responsibility and places it into Walter's black—not white, not Jewish—hands. *"My brother Walter is a determined man who can be hard if he has to be, but he is also a human being. It's because he's a human being that he believes that what you do, you do to advance the human race."* (p.327)
(see Coleman's Siblings, Ernestine, p.71)

Sex *whose obsession: Roth's or his readers'?*

No discussion of Philip Roth and his work is complete without a look at his views on sex. In the past, Roth has been accused of being preoccupied with sex, but in fact his work represents society's preoccupation with sex. Through his long career, Roth has personally moved through several stages of sexual behavior and understanding, all the way from **Portnoy's Complaint** to this novel, **The Human Stain**. His views reflect and parallel the stages of life he has had the pleasure of living through. His recurring theme clearly portrays how we are ever marked (stained) by our sexual nature. In this novel, Roth uses Coleman, and the Clinton sidebar, to further illustrate that a fixation or focus on sex is uniquely human.

- For this reason, Roth has given us the relationship of Coleman and Faunia set against the notoriety of the Clinton/Lewinsky affair. Everyone, in and out of the novel, is obsessed with the Clinton/Lewinsky story. In a terrific scene (p.146 to 150), Coleman overhears the analysis of the relationship by three young faculty members:

> *If he can't read Monica Lewinsky, how can he read Saddam Hussein? If he can't read and outfox Monica Lewinsky, the guy shouldn't be president. There's genuine grounds for impeachment .... this girl has revealed more about America than anybody since Dos Passos. She stuck a thermometer up the country's ass.* (p.147, 148)

- Farley wonders why there are *"veterans sleeping in the street while that draft dodger was sleeping in the White House? ... Slick Willie .... Lying about sex?"* (p.247)

- While it is true that Roth has always been obsessed with sex, we sense that in this novel, he is facing a change in perspective. Zuckerman has had prostate cancer, the treatment of which has rendered him impotent. He is no longer a player in the sexual arena. This has left him open to observing the sexual nature of others, enjoying their sensuality without worry about the rest of it. (see Dance, p.47)

> *How can one say, "No, this isn't a part of life," since it always is? The contaminant of sex, the redeeming corruption that de-idealizes the species and keeps us everlastingly mindful of the matter we are.* (p.37)

The Power of Language

Roth's other passion is the theory, process, and outcome of writing. He uses writing to name, describe, untangle, analyze, and understand the many facets of human behavior. He is especially concerned with the precision of words: how they label, identify, classify, and how they can fool the reader (or listener) through the subtle differences in interpretation.

- Everyone in **The Human Stain** writes something: Steena writes a poem, Faunia keeps a diary, Delphine composes illusionary emails, Coleman wants to write (or have written for him) a book about himself. Zuckerman is the writer/teller of this story. The process of writing is a dilemma, much like Delphine's *"dying to be seen and fear of being exposed."* As Zuckerman/Roth says,

    Writing personally is exposing and concealing at the same time ... Your book [is] your life ... (p.345)

- It is no accident that Roth puts thoughts about writing into the mouth of Coleman's father, who taught his children that *"things had classifications. They learned the power of naming precisely."* (p.93)

- Mr. Silk, senior, tries to teach them that word labels can have powerful dual purposes: to identify or to hurt. Coleman flippantly but innocently misapplies this lesson in the classroom with the label "spooks": *"Does anyone know these people? Do they exist or are they spooks?"* (p.6)

- When Coleman casually drops the word into the air, its effect spreads beyond his control. His father would be extremely disappointed at his carelessness. Coleman's ill-considered choice of words has the power to create a catastrophe of cataclysmic proportions: he ends up losing his job (his position of power) and his wife, who dies. (see Wordplay, p.51)

WRITING STRUCTURE

The First 85 Pages

Greek Drama

WRITING STRUCTURE

The First 85 Pages   *A Greek drama in modern times*

Roth has successfully and simultaneously merged the classic Greek drama with the modern-age drama, and he has done it in eighty-five pages. The structure of this opening section is tight and intricate. Every character, event, and parallel that appears later in the novel is dealt with here.

- **The Human Stain** opens by placing us into an exact moment in time – the summer of 1998. Roth mentions two historical events that serve as the backdrop to his story of Coleman Silk: a) the magical story of how two baseball giants, Sammy Sosa and Mark McGuire, one brown and one white, set new world home-run records; and b) the real-life story of Bill Clinton and Monica Lewinsky, a story that reads like a novel. Both of these stories echo throughout the book.

- First, Roth's almost trivial mention of this *"mythical battle between a home-run god who was white and a home-run god who was brown"* (p.2) is in reality a preamble to the mythical battle of epic proportion that is Coleman's battle with himself: his two halves, his black and his white. For Roth, nothing is insignificant and nothing is merely black or white.

- Second, Bill and Monica were engaged in a secret affair; so are Coleman and Faunia. In both stories, the age difference is significant. In both stories, Roth is highlighting people's insatiable thirst for the kind of judgmental speculation and curiosity that leads to the revelation of secrets, right down to *"every last mortifying detail."* (p.2)

- Roth uses the Clinton saga to reinforce Delphine's point that *"everyone knows"* (p.38) and points out that timing is everything. It is all about who finds out what and when, and what the consequences are of confronting a secret. Clinton's secret could not stay that way forever. The parallel to Coleman's secret, therefore, becomes self-evident.

- The Clinton story helps to frame this novel and remind us that sanctimonious attitudes lead to all kinds of perverse or pious judgments. The time of the impeachment trial reminds us that this was a time *"when the smallness of people was simply crushing, when some kind of demon had been unleashed in the nation."* (p.3) This is evident by the fact that the public outrage over Clinton's behavior outranked the outrage over the pronouncement of Khomeini's death sentence on Salman Rushdie. In effect, Coleman's behavior in the classroom was judged as equally heinous.

- Roth's critical questions are endless and set against the multiple layers of his observations. Roth asks why people can illogically rank the act of adultery (Clinton's or Coleman's) as more significant and insidious than the act of terrorism and murder. Roth is concerned about why no one remembers that Clinton (or Coleman) is "A HUMAN BEING [WHO] LIVES HERE." (p.3) After all, Roth reminds us, a human being is not a god. This leads us to the next major structural device that Roth uses: the characteristics found in classical Greek mythology and drama.

Greek Drama

The first eighty-five-page section functions like a classic Greek chorus that introduces, comments upon, and interprets the story's plot as it unfolds. Once the introduction is presented, we are ready to begin. This section is summed up: *"One last look at Athena, and then let the disgrace be complete."* (p.85)

- The single narrator of the novel is Nathan, whose life has taken an unexpected sexual turn. It is traditional for the narrator in a Greek drama to be a eunuch, an asexual and impotent character. Nathan is Roth's eunuch. The chorus is comprised of the individual characters in the novel, who stand behind the narrator. (see Narrator, p.54)

- As dramatists, the Greeks were interested in seeing people for the flawed and imperfect creatures they are. Unlike the biblical portrayal of a righteous, all-powerful God, the Greeks created their gods in the image of man. This is equally true of all of Roth's characters. They have deep flaws and not one is more righteous than another.

- A typical Greek hero is someone who feels bigger than ordinary folks and Coleman, the professor of Greek and Roman classics at Athena College, certainly falls victim to the pride of believing that he is above all other ordinary people. He believes that he can rise above the limitations set on him by the life that fate has handed him. He sets himself up for the inevitable classic fall because he wants to be *"free on a scale unimaginable to his father .... Free to go ahead and be stupendous."* (p.109) For him, there's no reason to *"accept a life on any other terms."* (p.121)

- The gods of Greek tragedy are concerned with how easily mere mortals betray themselves and each other through false pride, or "hubris." Coleman betrays his family and wife; Farley betrays Faunia and Coleman; Faunia is betrayed by Farley, Delphine, and Coleman's children; Delphine betrays herself and Coleman.

- There is a strong connection between pride and retribution, which leads to the downfall of the hero. When our flawed heroes try to defy their respective fates, they are punished. Roth portrays modern society as the "god" that requires punishment. Everyone demands vengeance against Coleman (and let's not forget Bill Clinton) for his perceived crimes.

- There are a great many other references in the novel to classic Greek drama.
    - Coleman teaches at Athena College.
    - Roth refers pointedly to Agamemnon (a ruler) and Achilles (a man who felt he was a god), who fight over a nameless girl. Similarly, Coleman and Farley fight over Faunia.

      ... a brutal quarrel over a young girl and her young body ... (p.5)
    - Delphine's name refers to the Oracle of Delphi, the priestess of prophecy. Delphine makes her prophecy known with the general and all-encompassing statement, *"Everyone knows."* (p.38)

- In the story of Oedipus, written by Sophocles in his play "Oedipus the King," Laius, the childless King of Thebes, goes to Delphi to ask if he will ever have a son. He is answered in the affirmative but is told that the son will be responsible for his father's death and will be driven out in turn by his own sons. In the same way, Coleman is indirectly responsible for the fate of his mother, who died of a broken heart; and he is directly abandoned by his son, Jeff, who refuses to listen to him; by his son, Mark, who accuses Coleman of Iris's death; and even by his beloved daughter, Lisa, who won't allow him to defend himself.

- The epigraph at the beginning of Sophocles' "Oedipus the King" reads:

    (Oedipus): What is the rite of purification? How shall it be done?

    (Creon): By banishing a man, or expiation of blood by blood...

SYMBOLS

Human Stain

Labels

Prince, The Crow

The Dance

SYMBOLS

The Human Stain

Everything in the novel leads directly to the concept of the human stain, which is both a theme and an image.

- The physical image of a mark or a stain stems back to biblical times or before, when people needed a way to show the negative side of human nature. Roth uses a stain, or outwardly identifiable mark, in this sense. Examples of marks are the mark of Cain, the color of one's skin, or the visible stain on Monica Lewinsky's blue dress.

- The Greeks took the symbolic image of a mark or stain and by converting it into a mask were able to show the idea of something concealed: a false appearance, or a secret. Every character in the novel is masked and has something to hide. Each character has his/her own personal perspective of what constitutes a human stain:
    - For Mark: the lack of an identifiable family history and therefore the denial of one's people and background
    - For Walt: Coleman's denial of his people and background
    - For Lisa: the inability to read
    - For Faunia: the need to hide her ability to read
    - For Ernestine: people's disposition for hatred
    - For Farley: his hatred of everyone

- Coleman alone seems oblivious to the idea of a covering mark or stain on himself. However, by trying to live life on his terms, he uses his mask, or false identity, to inadvertently cause harm to everyone he dearly loves. This is his human stain.

- While literature traditionally explores the mystery of human nature, Faunia states this novel's main premise: it's "okay" to just accept who we are. We're simply different, simply flawed, simply human, and we will always be marked by the efforts to overcome those flaws.

Labels

Labels are the identification marks that are used to classify our universal, yet individual, differences. Everyone uses them. (see Wordplay, p.51)

Roth considers this from several points of view:

- First: Why is it necessary to describe or categorize someone as a black, a Jew, or as anything else? Can outward physical markers really tell us about the individual and personal circumstances that influence one's personality or actions?

- Second: Invisible labels, such as "Vietnam vet" can have negative associations. Knowing this, Roth asks why we continue to use them.

- There is contempt for Faunia's perceived illiteracy and for her relationship with Coleman. Roth asks why this illiteracy is her fault. Why should anyone be concerned with Coleman's affair with Faunia? Their relationship is not adulterous in the way of Clinton's relationship with Monica. What is the purpose of such labels?

- Furthermore, labels did not help Coleman in the classroom when he uttered those fateful words: *"Does anyone know these people? Do they exist or are they spooks?"* (p.6) Coleman was *"undone by the perfect word."* (p.84) He was beaten down by a label. *"With words. With speech."* (p.92) Coleman's black students were not physically present in the classroom. They were not visible; they were just a name. How could Coleman tell from a name that they were black? Language can be precise, but labels can mislead and Coleman, who should know better, is fooled by the very precision of the language he loves.

- The idea of labeling the things that mark our individuality is also strongly illustrated by Coleman's son, Mark, (note the name) who relentlessly seeks to understand the genetic markers that make up his "Jewish" identity. He views the changing of the family name, their label, as a betrayal to the origins of that family.

- To understand the complexity of the imagery of labels requires the understanding that the nature of a mark or label or stain is ultimately a cover for something else. Roth leads us through a series of events up to Coleman's untimely end. The final symbol of the human stain is the thing that life itself covers up: death. We are all marked for eventual death.

Prince, The Crow

- The crow is an effective symbol for humanity. Crows are noisy and territorial, just like people. And just like people, they like to collect things and are often fooled by false first impressions and shiny exteriors. Faunia has befriended Prince, the big black crow with the strut (think of Coleman) who isolates himself from his crow community. As a misfit herself, Faunia understands that some crows, like some people, just never fit in. Even within a crow community, some crows isolate themselves. In this sense, Prince, Faunia's crow, is no different than Faunia herself, Farley, or even Coleman.

- Faunia identifies Prince as marked by his differences, and therefore he helps to add insight to Roth's concept of the human stain. Roth uses the crow as a symbol of the psychological phenomenon of "imprinting," which in nature means that a newborn animal will adopt as its mother the first thing it comes into contact with upon birth. Therefore a duck can believe that a human being is its mother. The duck is now marked for life. Furthermore, the idea of imprinting means that people can mark or change the natural relationships between living creatures. This implies randomness in the midst of natural order. It is the understanding that despite all efforts to the contrary, the human stain is often a natural consequence of life.

> *"That's what comes of being hand-raised .... That's what comes of hanging around all his life with people like us. The human stain," she said .... we leave a stain, we leave a trail, we leave our imprint .... Nothing to do with grace or salvation or redemption. It's in everyone. Indwelling. Inherent. Defining. The stain that is there before its mark. Without the sign it is there. The stain so intrinsic it doesn't require a mark .... All she was saying about the stain was that it's inescapable.* (p.242)

The Dance *the joy of human connection*

- Despite the seeming pessimism of the novel, there is a sense of respect for the simple act of being alive. The image of dance is used several times to give us a natural expression of human joy. Sad people dance around life; happy people dance through life.

- Roth uses this image to connect Steena and Faunia, both of whom Coleman calls Voluptas. (see Faunia, p.16) Through their respective dances, both Steena and Faunia come to a level of expression of freedom that neither has experienced before. For each, the most liberating time of life turns out to be through their relationship with Coleman.

> *[Steena] ... began what Coleman liked to describe as the single most slithery dance ever performed by a Fergus Falls girl ... she could have raised Gershwin himself from the grave with that dance ...* (p.115)

> *[Faunia] She laughs the easy laugh. And dances. Without the idealism, without the idealization, without*

the utopianism of the sweet young thing, despite everything she knows reality to be, despite the irreversible futility that is her life, despite all the chaos and callousness, she dances! (p.233)

- While Nathan doesn't dance for Coleman, he does dance with him. It is the dance that is liberating for him as well.

    Coleman said, "Want to dance?"

    I laughed ... this was not the savage, embittered, embattled avenger of Spooks, estranged from life and maddened by it – this was not even another man. This was another soul. What the hell, I thought, we'll both be dead soon enough, so I got up, and there on the porch Coleman Silk and I began to dance the fox trot together. (p.24, 25)

    On we danced. There was nothing overtly carnal in it ... [it was only] a thoughtless delight in just being alive ... (p.26)

WRITING STYLE
Wordplay
Narrator (Nathan Zuckerman)

WRITING STYLE

Wordplay *the use and placement of words*

- The important and obvious point is that the word "spook" has two dictionary meanings. First, "spook" is both a noun and a verb, related to ghosts or fright; secondly, "spook" is a negative reference to black people. This is the irony for Coleman:

    ... that one word did it. By no means the English language's most inflammatory, most heinous, most horrifying word, and yet word enough to lay bare, for all to see, to judge, to find wanting, the truth of who and what I am. (p.79)

- Coleman is accused of using a word that identifies and portrays blacks in a negative light, but no one realizes that Coleman himself is black. This incident clearly shows Roth's strong dislike for the abuse of language. He especially hates language that is compromised by things like euphemisms and political correctness. That is another reason he uses the Bill Clinton/ Monica Lewinsky story – as a historical marker of the art of language spinning.

- A second wonderful example of the power of language is given in the last scene of the book, where Roth plays with the words "auger," and "augur." One is a tool used for making holes; the other is both a noun – a soothsayer/prophet – or a verb meaning to predict or to foreshadow the future.

- Farley and Nathan are alone out on the ice and beside Farley lies a tool for ice fishing – an auger. The mood of the scene is cool and is unfolded with the care one would take if one were crossing thin ice. In fact, Zuckerman is very careful not to heat Farley up. Roth juxtaposes the meanings and intentions of these homonyms. Because an auger, the tool, can physically open the way to something else (i.e., drill a hole in the ice), it can also metaphorically lead the way to new conclusions and is therefore an effective tool for predicting or interpreting things, such as human behavior. However, as a tool in the hands of someone with the wrong intentions, an auger can cause great damage, such as in Farley's hands.

- There is a wonderful tension in this scene because, aside from the isolated position in which Zuckerman finds himself, Zuckerman suddenly realizes that Farley is responsible for the deaths of Coleman and Faunia:

    Here we are alone up where we are and I know, and he knows I know. And the auger knows. All ye know and all ye need to know, all inscribed in the spiral of its curving steel blade. (p.354)

- We nervously read on to find out whether Farley will hurt Nathan with this weapon. Against the backdrop of nature, peace, and silence, we are left to wonder if Nathan will end his days as a human stain on the landscape.

- It's a long and multilayered story that has brought us to this ice field, and Roth uses the curve of the spiral blade of the auger to show how we usually go in circles in order to get to the straight truth. Roth doesn't need to use a real "augur" or Delphic prophet to foretell or foreshadow the future – he accomplishes the same thing by merely using the image of the word's companion: the "auger," the tool.

- Zuckerman himself sums up Roth's discussion about writing. We have Farley, like Coleman before him, who just wants to tell someone his story. He finds Zuckerman, "the author," is the ideal choice for someone who will appreciate what Farley has been through and how he got to where he is and will record it without being judgmental.

    "What were you like before you went into the service?" Zuckerman asks Farley.

    "Is this for your book?"

    "Yes. Yes." I laughed out loud. ... "It's all for my book." (p.357)

    "What's the name of one of your books?"

    "The Human Stain."

    "Yeah? Can I get it?"

    "It's not out yet. It's not finished yet." (p.356)

- Because Zuckerman's/Roth's book is about ordinary people and their problems, it is and probably will forever remain an unfinished story.

Narrator   *Nathan Zuckerman*

- Nathan Zuckerman is the novel's narrator/storyteller, the writer/recorder, and the link to the major characters; therefore, he is the observer/interpreter of their words and behavior. He is Roth's "alter-brain." Coleman wants Nathan to write his story because he is a professional writer and professional writers, like Zuckerman/Roth, have credibility. Coleman can't do it himself because *"if he wrote the story ... nobody would believe it."* (p.11)

- At first Nathan objects because he has the wrong perception of Coleman: to him Coleman appears to be a misguided, misjudged, widowed, frustrated, and angry Jewish professor, who is having a hard time dealing with his particular stage in life. When Nathan later discovers that Coleman has a completely different story to tell, he becomes interested and says, *"I was completely seized by his story, by its end and by its beginning, and, then and there, I began this book."* (p.337)

- As he has done in some of his other novels, notably **The Counterlife**, Roth likes to start at the end of a story in order to get at the beginning. Then he fills in the middle and blurs the lines between narrator and author.

- The narrator of a story is the person we traditionally rely on for our facts and our perspective. In Roth's novels, this is never a simple issue. Clearly Nathan is the novel's narrator; after all, **The Human Stain** is written in the first person, in Nathan's voice. But Nathan knows none of the true facts about Coleman until three-quarters of the way through the book. In fact, we, as readers, know the true facts before he does. This places Zuckerman in a strange position and leads Roth to ask important questions about the validity of the narrator.

- Our narrator, Nathan, doesn't know Coleman (or anyone) well. He has his own problems and wants strongly to be reclusive. Nathan only knows what he knows by using his imagination, and he tells us so. As a writer, and as a narrator, he hands us what Philip Roth likes to call a "varnished truth."
- Finally, in considering the validity of the narrator and what he knows or doesn't know, we have to return to Delphine's prophetic utterance, *"Everyone knows."* (p.38) Although everyone has used this statement at some time or other, Roth/Zuckerman tells us not to be so sure about what we know:

    Because we don't know, do we? ... What we know is that, in an unclichéd way, nobody knows anything. You can't know anything. The things you know you don't know. Intention? Motive? Consequence? Meaning? All that we don't know is astonishing. Even more astonishing is what passes for knowing. (p.208, 209)

    But still Roth doesn't drop the subject. He again asks the question,

    How did such a man as Coleman come to exist? What is it that he was? Was the idea he had for himself of lesser validity or of greater validity than someone else's idea of what he was supposed to be? Can such things even be known? (p.333)

- Then, in typical Roth fashion, he answers the questions. He tells us that Coleman was a man who was fooled by the unpredictability of other humans and of time.

    [He was] ... ensnared by the history he hadn't quite counted on .... [by] the present moment, the common lot, the current mood, the mind of one's country, the stranglehold of history that is one's own time. Blindsided by the terrifyingly provisional nature of everything. (p.335, 336)

- In other words, he is blindsided by the one thing from which we can never escape: our **Human Stain**.

LAST THOUGHTS

Author Background

The Other Roth

Works by Roth

Other Characters

LAST THOUGHTS

Author Background

- Philip Roth was born March 19, 1933, in Newark, New Jersey, as the younger of two sons to Herman and Bess Roth. He was raised in a secular Jewish family within a secular Jewish community comprised mostly of grandchildren of turn-of-the-century Polish and Russian Jewish immigrants. Here is where Roth's passion for baseball and where the East-and-West process of assimilation began: *"[Jewish] religious orthodoxy was only beginning to be seriously eroded by American life."* (Roth's Book, My Life as a Man)

- In 1954, Roth attended Bucknell University in Pennsylvania where he discovered literature and attained his B.A. He got his Master's degree at the University of Chicago, and there he began teaching English. He also taught comparative literature at the University of Pennsylvania and creative writing at Iowa University and at Princeton. His last teaching post was at Hunter College, New York; he retired from teaching in 1992. Roth describes his first marriage, to a non-Jewish girl, as horrific. After they separated in 1962, Roth went through intensive therapy that ended when she died in 1968 in a car crash. Roth says in his book, **The Facts,**

    Without doubt she was my worst enemy ever ... but she was also nothing less than the greatest creative-writing teacher of them all, specialist par excellence in the aesthetics of extremist fiction ... Zuckerman ... was right when he said I owe everything to an alcoholic shiksa.

- This is not the only time that Roth quotes Nathan Zuckerman about facts of his own life. He calls Zuckerman his "alter-brain," rather than alter ego, and lifts him above the written page to mythical, "Harvey-the rabbit" status. Zuckerman is the ultimate imaginary friend.

- Roth's next major relationship was with the actress Claire Bloom. They lived together in London, England, and had homes in Connecticut and Vermont from 1976 until the late nineties. Many of his books during this period were set partially in England. Their relationship had a very stormy ending, which culminated in a hateful portrayal of Roth in Bloom's autobiography, **Leaving The Doll House.** He responded with the character, Eve, in **I Married a Communist.**

- His fascination with writing and the promotion of writers has lasted throughout his life. In 1974 he began a book series called **Writers of the Other Europe,** and he served as its general editor until 1989. Through this series he introduced authors from behind the iron curtain and others such as Bruno Schultz, Milan Kundera, Primo Levi, Ivan Klima, and Aharon Appelfeld.

- Roth has made Connecticut his main home since 1973 and describes it as a place where *"there's not much else to do except write."* This is echoed in **The Human Stain** when Zuckerman says, *"It's my job. It's all I do."* (p.213)

- It is known that Roth, like Zuckerman, has had surgery for prostate cancer. He makes an earlier reference to this in his book **The Counterlife** where Henry, Zuckerman's brother, took heart medication that interfered with his *"sexual function."*

- In **The Human Stain**, Zuckerman (Roth) says:

    I want to make it clear that it wasn't impotence that led me into a reclusive existence. ... [it was that] .... I couldn't meet the costs of its clamoring anymore, could no longer marshal the wit, the strength, the patience, the illusion, the irony, the ardor, the egoism, the resilience—or the toughness, or the shrewdness, or the falseness, the dissembling, the dual being, the erotic professionalism—to deal with its array of misleading and contradictory meanings. (p.36, 37)

    Leave it to Roth to bring into service every noun he knows in order to describe his situation.

- This brings up a final point about Roth and his personal and professional development. The subjects and philosophies that Roth has investigated in his numerous books represent his age and stage of life at the time of writing. It is fascinating to observe how many of Roth's viewpoints have evolved, intensified, or been modified as his perspective and thinking changed.

- Roth has a unique capacity to see where he is currently standing and where he has come from. In addition, he has the vision to contemplate where he is going. It is interesting that Roth uses Ernestine, and not Zuckerman, to make the point that personal views are especially dangerous when they are static. (This is also presented in **American Pastoral** and **I Married a Communist**.)

  > *... he was Coleman all the way. Set out to do it and did it. That was the extraordinary thing about him from the time he was a boy—that he stuck to a plan completely ....*
  >
  > *All the lying that was necessitated by the big lie, to his family, to his colleagues, and he stuck to it right to the end. Even to be buried as a Jew.*
  >
  > *... Coleman did this when he was .... a firecracker of 27. But he wasn't going to be 27 forever. It wasn't going to be 1953 forever. People age. Nations age. Problems age. Sometimes they age right out of existence.* (p.325, 326)

The Other Philip Roth

- In order to fully appreciate Roth's body of writing, and with apologies to Nathan Zuckerman, it is important to try to isolate the real Philip Roth from the way Philip Roth is perceived. This can be done by asking the following questions:
    - Is Roth still the self-obsessed and narrow thinker? Is he still *"the Jersey boy with the dirty mouth who writes the books Jews love to hate?"* (Counterlife)
    - Or is he the powerful observer with *"the writer's sense of reality ...[who] transforms into writing ... (whatever catastrophe turns up)?"* (p.170, The Human Stain)
    - Or is he the brilliant narrator, a master at telling the "human" story with all its facets and in all its complexity? Even though the reader may get lost in an individual passage, Roth never loses the thread.

- Through his many novels we see a deepening progression in Roth's understanding of himself and a gradual acceptance of his role in the world as a Jew. In the very early days of his writing career, it didn't occur to him that his life as a Jew would make interesting literature, but when he realized that through his humor he could deal with what his Jewishness meant to him, he began to structure his themes around it.

- In the beginning, Roth definitely did not see himself as a defender of the Jews and wrote a story, "The Defender of the Jews," which appears in his first book, **Goodbye, Columbus**. In **Portnoy's Complaint**, he then contemplated how the Jewish male tries to find ways to express his Jewishness in ways that are acceptable to himself.

- Next he moved to a broader view of the Jew in general when he realized that there is nothing strange about being Jewish. In fact *"... there is nothing more to say than there (is) about having two arms and two legs. It would (seem) strange not to be Jewish – stranger still, to hear someone announce that he wished he weren't a Jew or that he intended not to be in the future."* (My Life as a Man)

- In **The Human Stain**, Roth has moved outside the boundaries of individual culture to a place where he can contemplate how all people (whether Jew, Black, white, male, female) can express themselves.

- Perhaps it could be concluded that in spite of their sarcastic language and observations both Philip Roth and Nathan Zuckerman have mellowed and matured into more spiritual and accepting human beings. While they haven't lost their bite, they are more accepting of life as it is and as it gives. After all, an earlier Roth/Zuckerman could never have danced so innocently with another man. An earlier Roth/Zuckerman might never have considered the beauty of life and nature while at the same time observing Farley, a man who just got away with murder. The novel ends when Nathan takes a last look at Farley and sees in him only a man.

    ... the only human marker in all of nature ... Only rarely, at the end of our century, does life offer up a vision as pure and peaceful as this one: a solitary man on a bucket, fishing through eighteen inches of ice in a lake that's constantly turning over its water atop an arcadian mountain in America. (p.361)

- This is *"if not the whole story, the whole picture"* of humanity, stains included. (p.361)

- A prediction can be made that, like the water that is constantly turning itself over on this mountain top, Roth will return to tell the same story once again, but in a new, brilliantly unique way.

Works by Roth

Goodbye, Columbus; Five Short Stories (1959).

Letting Go (1962).

When She Was Good (1967)

Portnoy's Complaint (1969)

Our Gang (1971)

The Breast (1972)

The Great American Novel (1973)

My Life As a Man (1974)

Reading Myself and Others (1975) (non-fiction)

The Professor of Desire (1977)

The Ghost Writer (1979)

A Philip Roth Reader (1980)

Zuckerman Unbound (1981)

The Anatomy Lesson (1983)

Zuckerman Bound: A Trilogy and Epilogue (1985)

The Counterlife (1986)

The Facts: A Novelist's Autobiography (1988) (non-fiction)

Deception: A Novel (1990)

Patrimony: A True Story (1991) (non-fiction)

Operation Shylock: A Confession (1993)

Sabbath's Theater (1995)

American Pastoral (1997)

I Married a Communist (1998)

The Human Stain (2000)

The Dying Animal (2001)

The Plot Against America (2004)

Everyman (2006)

Exit Ghost (2007)

Awards

Second prize in the O. Henry Prize Story Contest of 1960 for "Defender of the Faith."

National Book Award for Fiction in 1960 for **Goodbye, Columbus**

National Book Critics Circle Award in 1987 for **The Counterlife**

National Book Critics Circle Award in 1992 for **Patrimony**

PEN/Faulkner Award for Fiction in 1993 for **Operation Shylock**

Time Magazine's Best American Novel of 1993 for **Operation Shylock**

National Book Award for Fiction in 1995 for **Sabbath's Theater**

Pulitzer Prize in 1998 for **American Pastoral**

Ambassador Book Award of the English-Speaking Union, 1998

National Medal of Arts at the White House, 1998

More About the Other Characters

Iris

- Iris, Coleman's *"non-Jewish Jewish Iris,"* (p.132) is the perfect cover for his secret. With her dark, kinky hair, Coleman would have had a reasonable explanation, had he needed it, for the "black" characteristics of his children.

- He chooses Iris over Steena, his perfect white soul mate, and even over Ellie, his perfect black soul mate, primarily because he likes to live on the edge: With Ellie, *"the whole thing lacks ambition."* With Iris, *"he has the secret again. And the gift to be secretive again .... Iris gives him back his life on the scale he wants to live it."* (p.135, 136)

- Coleman liked having a secret and was willing to sacrifice many things, including his mother and his siblings, in order to find a way to continue being secretive. By choosing Iris, Coleman finds his solution.

  > *[Iris becomes] the secret to his secret, flavored with just a drop of the ridiculous – the redeeming, reassuring ridiculous, life's little contribution to every human decision .... he now made sense.* (p.132)

- Coleman is also not above a little revenge. By marrying Iris, a Jewish girl, Coleman evens the score between Dr. Fensterman (see novel, p.33) and Coleman's father. Coleman's marriage to Iris is *"a colossal sui generis score-settling joke."* (p.131)

- Ironically, Iris was the one person who could have shared Coleman's secrets. As the daughter of self-styled Jewish anarchists, Iris would have helped Coleman fight for the right to live his secret. She would have instantly applied the idea of the Black struggle for freedom and equality to Coleman's idea of life, but he couldn't ever bring himself to tell her.

Steena and Ellie

- Steena and Ellie represent the idea of duality, the paradoxical nature of Coleman's personality: something that can be itself and its opposite at the same time. *"He could play his skin however he wanted, color himself just as he chose."* (p.109)

- Steena and Ellie can also be seen as forerunners of Faunia and Ernestine. Like Ernestine, Ellie is comfortable with her black identity. She represents the life that Coleman could have had as a black man within the borders of black society. Steena represents the difficulties of life in a mixed-race setting; Faunia represents other mixes: age, social class, and education.

- Through his relationships with Steena and Ellie, we see Coleman develop. At each of these stages in his life, he might have been able to settle down: *"Had Steena said fine, he would have lived another life."* (p.126) But Steena didn't have the kind of steely strength that would help her face the challenge of an interracial relationship at that time. With Ellie, he could have relaxed and been his "real" self, but life would have been boring. In the end, Coleman decides he misses the element of secrecy and danger. He meets Iris and *"he's back in the ring."* (p.135)

- Coleman might have been happy enough with either of these women, but something in the center of his being wouldn't allow it. He is the fighter who cannot *"retire undefeated."* (p.135) He needs to keep pushing the boundaries of his existence: *"All he'd ever wanted, from earliest childhood on, was to be free: not black, not even white – just on his own and free."* (p.120)

Coleman's Parents *The Silks*

- Coleman's father represents several ideas, such as fatherhood, literacy, and racism. Mr. Silk (no first name is ever given to him) is a victim of his times. Although he is a skilled professional, he lost his business as a result of the shattered economy of the Depression. As a black man, he was reduced to working as a waiter on the railroad. It was the most he could hope for.

- However, Mr. Silk is an educated man with an obsession for English language and literature. His favorite play is Shakespeare's *Julius Caesar* and he gives his children their true identities through their middle names.

    o Coleman Brutus: Brutus betrays his best friend and ally, Caesar, by dealing the first murderous blow. Coleman does the same to his family when he opts "out" as a white man.

    o Walter Antony: Marc Antony stands up for Caesar and gives him, posthumously, dignity and respect. Walter refuses to allow Coleman back into their lives and thus attempts to maintain the family's dignity and respect.

    o Ernestine Calpurnia: Calpurnia is the loyal wife of Caesar. Ernestine stays quietly loyal to both Walter and to Coleman.

- Mr. Silk is a stickler for the accuracy of language. He wants nothing to be misunderstood. All labels have to be specific and appropriate.

    He was very fussy about his children's speaking properly. Growing up, they never said, "See the bow-wow." They didn't even say, "See the doggie." They said, "See the Doberman. See the beagle. See the terrier." They learned things had classifications. They learned the power of naming precisely. (p.93)

He would have frowned upon Coleman's misuse of the label, *"spooks."* (p.6) (see Power of Language, p.31)

- Coleman's mother, Gladys, is the long-suffering, silently accepting, universal image of motherhood. Her skills as a nurse are considerable:

    .. there was no finer nurse on the hospital staff, no nurse more intelligent, knowledgeable, reliable, or capable than Mrs. Silk – and that included the nursing supervisor herself. (p.86)

- Her skills as a mother, especially as Coleman's mother, are also considerable.

    Coleman got what the patients got: her conscientious kindness and care. Coleman got just about anything he wanted. The father leading the way, the mother feeding the love. The old one-two. (p.95)

- Like all mothers, Gladys has hopes and dreams for Coleman's future. In light of this, what Coleman does with his life is exceptionally sad. Roth doesn't pull any punches.

    He was murdering her. You don't have to murder your father. The world will do that for you ... Who there is to murder is the mother, and that's what he saw he was doing to her, the boy who'd been loved as he'd been loved by this woman. Murdering her on behalf of his exhilarating notion of freedom! (p.138)

- And like all mothers, she sees clearly her child and his mistakes. Beneath the dreams she has no illusions, but she is helplessly caught in her role as parent and observer. She knows that Coleman is a victim of his age and ideals; he's twenty-seven when he makes the irrevocable decision to marry Iris and to "out" from his life as he knows it. There is nothing she can do or say that will change his destiny as he chooses it. He is searching for his *"alternate destiny ... Don't most people want to walk out of the fucking lives they've been handed?"* (p.139)

- He eventually discovers *"freedom is very dangerous. And nothing is on your own terms for long."* (p.145)

Coleman's Siblings *Ernestine and Walt*

- Ernestine is the supporter and Walt is the protector. Ernestine earnestly supports Coleman, while Walt protects their mother by setting up a wall between them. Throughout the years, Ernestine quietly keeps in contact with Coleman. She is his bridge to his former life. They call each other and report on significant life events: birthdays, marriages, children, deaths. She had *"never told anybody about it. Didn't see any reason to."* (p.319) Walt breaks all contact with Coleman and allows Gladys no contact with Coleman, because he thinks that is the best way to protect his mother.

- Ernestine describes the Silk men as being strong and decisive, and this is true of their father, Coleman, and Walter: *"These men make up their minds, and that's it. Well there was a price to pay for their decisiveness."* (p.321, 322) (see Revenge, p.28)

- Consistent with their father's emphasis on training in language and the arts, each of the Silk children (and the grandchildren: Lisa, Michael, and Jeff) became teachers. Whereas Coleman became Athena College's "white" Dean of Classics, Walter became the first colored teacher, principal, and superintendent of schools in the Asbury Park school system, a very white neighborhood. There is irony in the fact that Coleman's secret life made him run, duck, and zigzag; he was always fearful of being uncovered as a black in a white world. Walt, on the other hand, hid nothing and just moved forward successfully as a black in a white world.

- There is no racial stereotyping in the characters of Ernestine and Walt. Despite the sense of an uphill battle, Ernestine makes a strong case for human individuality.

    o Humanity: Hatred will get you nowhere, because *"the danger with hatred is, once you start in on it.... you can't stop. I don't know anything harder to control than hating."* (p.328)

    o First Amendment - freedom of speech: As her father's daughter, Ernestine is disturbed by the careless use of language: *"... the words that I hear spoken strike me as less and less of a description of what things really are."* Why should people have to be *"so terribly frightened of every word one uses?"* (p.328, 329)

    o Educational equality: Ernestine has an interesting perspective on education and feels that separating educational information into broad categories such as Black History Month widens the gap between people. A black explorer, such as Matthew Henson, should be studied in the same context of exploration as other explorers. All students should be given the benefit of knowing who, black or white, came before them and led them to where they are today. Nathan Zuckerman did not know who Matthew Henson was because he *"was not exposed to Black History Month as a youngster."* (p.329)

Coleman's Children   *Lisa, Mark, Jeff, Michael*

- Jeff and Michael, two college professors, each married with children, are not a major part of the story other than to illustrate Coleman's incredible luck at not being found "out" because of his children, and his isolation from them.

- Lisa and Mark, last-born twins, are the important parts of Coleman's life. They are the ones who marked him as "safe"; two for the price of one and they are not black. As twins, they represent the two sides of Coleman's life and his personality. Coleman is comfortable with one side of himself (Lisa) but not the other side (Mark). Coleman is comfortable with his accomplishments, but not with his secret.

- Lisa is a reading-recovery teacher for children who are having a difficult time learning how to read. She is a product of her background, but without the physical markings of color. She has her grandfather's love of language; she is as intense as Iris, but as kind and caring as Gladys. In her job, she is completely obsessed and as *"morally in over her head"* as Coleman. (p.58) She is completely thrown by the idea that a child might be unable to read: *" 'What do you do with a kid who can't read? Think of it .... It's difficult, Daddy. Your ego gets a little caught up in it, you know.'"* (p.59) With Faunia, Coleman finds out the answer to the question.

- Lisa and Coleman have always been very close, and so he is not prepared for Lisa's rejection. (p.60) On the other hand, Mark, Lisa's twin, and Coleman are intricately connected, but are not very close. Mark's name suggests the idea of one thing being imprinted on another. Of all Coleman's children, Mark has been stained by the negative elements of Coleman's life, such as Coleman's intense obsession to be something other than what he is, the intimidation he felt from his own father, and his rejection of his mother and siblings. Mark felt this intuitively and always pushed for the truth.

    Almost from the time he could speak, Mark couldn't give up the idea that his father was against him ...

    Because of his unshakable enmity for his father, Mark had made himself into whatever his family wasn't – more sadly to the point, into whatever he [Coleman] wasn't. (p.60, 61)

- Mark writes poetry about parents who wrong their children. In the case of Coleman, Mark is 100 percent right. Coleman has made up plausible family histories about the Silberzweigs, who originated in Russia. Iris and the other children believed him; Mark did not. Nathan understands this from his conversations with Ernestine.

    > ... *never forget that there was a lie at the foundation of his relationship to his children, a terrible lie, and that Markie had intuited it, somehow understood that the children, who carried their father's identity in their genes ... never had the complete knowledge of who they are and who they were.* (p.321)

- Because of Mark's very human and understandable frustrations and anger, Mark targets Coleman for what he is.

    > *You killed mother, the way you kill everything! Because you have to be right! Because you won't apologize, because every time you are a hundred percent right ...* (p.62)

- As readers, we see it too. Coleman never apologizes for the "spooks" incident, for wronging his mother, or for lying to Iris and his children. When he learns from a conversation with his son, Jeff, about all the misinformation about his relationship with Faunia, he gets angry and wants to know the source: *"'I want names. I want to know who this everyone is.'"* (p.173)

Nelson Primus

- Despite all of Coleman's efforts to pass seamlessly into the white community, his former life always rises up to confront him. Aside from the major irony of the "spooks" incident, Nelson represents another form of judgment on Coleman.

- Coleman has continually flaunted his real identity in an ironic way; for example, when he went out of his way to hire minorities, especially blacks. (He hired Herb Keble.) Coleman continues to flaunt himself by hiring Nelson Primus, a black lawyer, but even Nelson does not guess the truth about Coleman. Roth ingeniously and subtly installs Nelson into the story without actually identifying Nelson as black. He only drops very large hints.

    > *(Nelson's) cocky bluntness ... [reminds Coleman] of himself at Primus's age, because of a repugnance in Primus for sentimental nonessentials that he made no effort to disguise.* (p.75)

- Nelson's wife is a philosophy professor that Coleman himself hired. (p.75)

- Nelson is a *"sleekly good-looking, raven-haired young man .... a panther ready to pounce."* (p.75, 76)

- Nelson, like Walt, has nothing to hide and has succeeded on his own terms. He works behind a large desk *"whose surface epitomized the unsullied clean slate .... There'll be no spooks in Nelson Primus's life."* (p.78, 79)

- While Nelson is obviously fooled about Coleman's real identity, Coleman ironically rages at Nelson as if he were white, *"'I never again want to ... see your smug fucking lily-white face.'"* (p.81) Nelson says to his wife, *"'I don't fault him for unloading on me like that. But, honey, the question remains: why white?'"* (p.82)

Dr. Fensterman

- When Coleman and Dr. Fensterman's son were both vying for the position of class valedictorian, Dr. Fensterman presents himself as the instrument of opportunity for Coleman. In his wisdom, Dr. Fensterman *"knew that prejudice in academic institutions against colored students was far worse than it was against Jews."* (p.86)

- He offered Coleman's father influence to try to promote Gladys to the position of head nurse, and three thousand dollars for Coleman to use to get to college, in exchange for Coleman taking an academic "dive."

- Fensterman reasoned that Coleman, as the student in second position, would still be the *"highest-ranking colored student in the country, even in the state, [and therefore to graduate] as salutatorian rather than as valedictorian would make no difference whatsoever when he enrolled at Howard University."* (p.87) There was only one view open to Coleman (Howard University, not Princeton or Yale) and Dr. Fensterman would open the window so that Coleman could get there more easily. (The Yiddish word *fenster* means "window.")

Herb Keble

- The character of Herb Keble is a superb example of Roth's use of irony. When Coleman became Dean of Athena, he hired minorities and women. Herb Keble was *"the first black in anything other than a custodial position."* (p.16)

- When Coleman was looking for support in the "spooks" incident, Herb said, *"I can't be with you on this, Coleman. I'm going to have to be with them."* (p.16) Neither Herb, nor the reader at this point, knew that Coleman was a *"them."*

- At Coleman's funeral, Keble is still under the misapprehension that Coleman is white and Jewish. The irony continues to play back when he speaks and says he was wrong not to have backed Coleman in his struggle with the college. *"I should have said, 'I must be with you.' I should have worked to oppose his enemies ... so he could have taken heart at the expression of support ..."* (p.310)

- This is also an ironic poke at the Clinton-Lewinsky saga that Roth sets up at the beginning of the book. (see First 85 pages, p.35) In both sets of circumstances, the lack of public support stems from the all-too-human propensity (the human stain) to make quick, unsupported judgments from a position of moral indignation.

FROM THE NOVEL
Quotes

FROM THE NOVEL ...

Memorable Quotes from the Text of *The Human Stain*

PAGE 2. Ninety-eight in New England was a summer of exquisite warmth and sunshine, in baseball a summer of mythical battle between a home-run god who was white and a home-run god who was brown, and in America the summer of an enormous piety binge, a purity binge, when terrorism – which had replaced communism as the prevailing threat to the country's security – was succeeded by cocksucking, and a virile, youthful middle-aged president and a brash, smitten twenty-one-year-old employee carrying on in the Oval Office like two teenage kids in a parking lot revived America's oldest communal passion, historically perhaps its most treacherous and subversive pleasure: the ecstasy of sanctimony.

PAGE 12. There is something fascinating about what moral suffering can do to someone who is in no obvious way a weak or feeble person. It's more insidious even than what physical illness can do, because there is no morphine drip or spinal block or radical surgery to alleviate it. Once you're in its grip, it's as though it will have to kill you for you to be free of it. Its raw realism is like nothing else.

PAGE 19, 20. Now, most writers who are brought to a standstill after rereading two years' work – even one year's work, merely half a year's work—and finding it hopelessly misguided and bringing down on it the critical guillotine are reduced to a state of suicidal despair from which it can take months to begin to recover. Yet Coleman, by abandoning a draft of a book as bad as the draft he'd finished, had somehow managed to swim free not only from the wreck of the book but from the wreck of his life.

PAGE 45. This was how Coleman became my friend and how I came out from under the stalwartness of living alone in my secluded house and dealing with the cancer blows. Coleman Silk danced me right back into life ... here was a man who made things happen. Indeed, the dance that sealed our friendships was also what made his disaster my subject. And made his disguise my subject. And made the proper presentation of his secret my problem to solve ... I did no more than find a friend, and all the world's malice came rushing in.

PAGE 52. The sensory fullness, the copiousness, the abundant – superabundant – detail of life, which is the rhapsody. And Coleman and Faunia, who are now dead, deep in the flow of the unexpected, day by day, minute by minute, themselves details in that superabundance.

Nothing lasts, and yet nothing passes, either. And nothing passes just because nothing lasts.

PAGE 68, 69. He's just a crazy Vietnam vet. But he knows things, goddamnit. And she knows nothing. But do they put away the stupid bitch? They put him away ... And all he did was what they had trained him to do: you see the enemy, you kill the enemy. They train you for a year, then they try to kill you for a year, and when you're just doing what they trained you to do, that is when they fucking put the leather restraints on you and shoot you full of shit.

PAGE 85. Silky. Silky Silk. The name by which he had not been known for over fifty years ...

PAGE 96. "You're rolling with the punch, Mom ... Once, and only once, and only because I was a jerk, only because of my own stupid mistake ... did I get a little stunned."

With that remark, his father had heard enough. "I've seen men get hit with a punch that they never saw coming ... when that happens, it knocks them cold..."

PAGE 153, 154. It's as though not even that most basic level of imaginative thought had been admitted into consciousness to cause the slightest disturbance. A century of destruction unlike any other in its extremity befalls and blights the human race – scores of millions of ordinary people condemned to suffer deprivation upon deprivation, atrocity upon atrocity, evil upon evil, half the world or more subjected to pathological sadism as social policy, whole societies organized and fettered by the fear of violent persecution, the degradation of individual life engineered on a scale unknown throughout history, nations broken and enslaved by ideological criminals who rob them of everything, entire populations so demoralized as to be unable to get out of bed in the morning with the minutest desire to face the day ... all the terrible touchstones presented by this century, and here they are up in arms about Faunia Farley. Here in America either it's Faunia Farley or it's Monica Lewinsky! ... This, in 1998, is the wickedness they have to put up with.

PAGE 183. Because of his credo, because of his insolent, arrogant "I am not one of you, I can't bear you, I am not part of your Negro we" credo. The great heroic struggle against their we – and look at what he now looked like! ... Is there where you've come, Coleman, to seek the deeper meaning of existence? A world of love, that's what you had, and instead you forsake it for this! The tragic, reckless thing that you've done! And not just to yourself—to us all. To Ernestine. To Walt. To Mother. To me [Coleman's father]. To me in my grave ... What else grandiose are you planning, Coleman Brutus? Whom next are you going to mislead and betray?

PAGE 290. Simply to make the accusation is to prove it. To hear the allegation is to believe it. No motive for the perpetrator is necessary, no logic or rationale is required. Only a label is required. The label is the motive. The label is the evidence. The label is the logic. Why did Coleman Silk do this? Because he is an x, because he is a y, because he is both. First a racist and now a misogynist. It is too late in the century to call him a Communist, though that is the way it used to be done ...That explains everything. That and the craziness ... [of being human].

PAGE 306, 307. It was strange to think ... that people so well-educated and professionally civil should have fallen so willingly for the venerable human dream of a situation in which one man can embody evil. Yet there is this need, and it is undying and it is profound.

PAGE 315, 316. There is truth and then again there is truth. For all that the world is full of people who go around believing they've got you or your neighbor figured out, there really is no bottom to what is not known. The truth about us is endless. As are the lies. Caught between, I thought. Denounced by the high-minded, reviled by the righteous – then exterminated by the criminally crazed ... whipsawed, I thought ... By the antagonism that is the world.

ACKNOWLEDGEMENTS

ACKNOWLEDGEMENTS

Adachi, Ken. "Is anyone out there actually reading?" *Toronto Star*, Saturday Magazine. Sept. 17, 1988.

Books & Writers, "Philip (Milton) Roth." Amazon.com. 2000. www.kirjasto.sci.fi

Kakutani, Michiko. "Confronting the Failures of a Professor who Passes." New York Times on the Web, May 2, 2000. http://www.nytimes.com

Marchand, Philip. "A case of the dummy and the ventriloquist." The *Toronto Star,* Saturday Magazine. March 31, 1990.

McGrath, Charles. "Zuckerman's Alter Brain." New York Times on the Web, May 7, 2000. http://www.nytimes.com

Roth, Philip. *The Facts: A Novelist's Autobiography.* New York: Farrar, Straus and Giroux, 1988.

The Random House Dictionary of the English Language. The Unabridged Edition. New York: Random House, 1966.

RECEIVED NOV 26 2010 /1995

DISCARD